A Gift For:

From:

MUSEUM

How to Use Your Interactive Story Buddy™:

1. Activate your Story Buddy by pressing the "On / Off" button on the ear.
2. Read the story aloud in a quiet place. Speak in a clear voice when you see the highlighted phrases.
3. Listen to your Story Buddy respond with several different phrases throughout the book.

Clarity and speed of reading affect the way Mason™ responds. He may not always respond to young children.

Watch for even more Interactive Story Buddy characters.
For more information, visit us on the Web at Hallmark.com/StoryBuddy.

Copyright © 2012 Hallmark Licensing, LLC

Published by Hallmark Gift Books, a division
of Hallmark Cards, Inc., Kansas City, MO 64141
Visit us on the Web at Hallmark.com.

Editorial Director: Carrie Bolin
Editor: Jennifer Snuggs
Art Director: Chris Opheim
Designer: Scott Swanson
Production Designer: Dan Horton

ISBN:978-1-59530-543-5
KOB1049

Printed and bound in China
NOV12

I Reply TECHNOLOGY ™ Hallmark's **I Reply Technology** brings your Story Buddy™ to life! When you read the key phrases out loud, your Story Buddy™ gives a variety of responses, so each time you read feels as magical as the first.

BOOK 2

MASON

Visits the Zoo

Written by Bill Gray
Illustrated by Scott Brown

Hallmark

Mason the teddy bear and his friend, Jacob, were enjoying a day at the zoo.

"My, what a handsome spotted leopard!" Mason whispered to Jacob from the opening in Jacob's backpack. The little bear enjoyed seeing new things.

Jacob saw a sign that read, "SEAL SHOW."
"Cool!" he shouted. "Come on, Mason! We have
half an hour before we have to meet Mom and
Dad at the gift shop."

Jacob sat on a long bench by the seal pool and placed his backpack on the ground. Mason could hear seals splashing, but all he could see were feet. Mason quickly became bored.

Suddenly, the little bear heard laughter
coming from outside the seal show.
"Wee! This is fun!" a voice giggled.
This made Mason curious.

Mason carefully climbed out of Jacob's backpack and followed the laughter to a large exhibit full of monkeys.

"Hi! I'm Mickey! Want to play?" chuckled a monkey on a tire swing.

"Pleased to meet you, Mickey. I'm Mason."

"Come on in and let's be friends!" Mickey said. The little bear was all about making new friends.

Mason thought he was small enough to squeeze through the bars of the exhibit, but he got stuck. "Oh, dear!" he exclaimed.

"Don't worry," said Mickey. "I'll help!"
Mickey pulled on the bear's arm until he popped through. They both tumbled to the ground, rolling with laughter. Laughing made Mason sunny inside.

In the monkey exhibit, Mickey and Mason played "swing on a tire," "hide behind a rock," and "throw things at the tree."

"You're really fun to monkey around with," said Mickey.
"You're fun as well!" Mason giggled. Playing was one of
the little bear's best things to do.

While the two friends played, Mason spied what looked like
a small tunnel in a nearby hill.

"Want to see where that goes?" asked Mickey.

"Gee . . . I'm not sure . . . " said Mason. "Tunnels are a bit scary."

"Not this one!" Mickey reassured him. "Take my hand!"
Mason slowly took Mickey's hand, and they walked into
the dark tunnel. Mason didn't like dark places.

Thankfully, the darkness quickly turned into sunlight as the two made their way through the short tunnel and into the elephant exhibit.

"See! No problem!" Mickey said, and he quickly waved goodbye and disappeared into the tunnel.

As Mason waved goodbye to Mickey, he noticed something on his fur. "Oh, my! I'm covered in tunnel dirt!"

"I can help with that," said a deep voice from behind. A helpful elephant immediately put his trunk in a bucket, filled it with water, and raised it toward Mason.

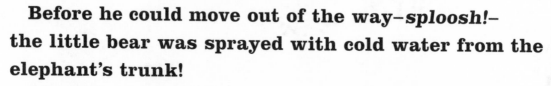

Before he could move out of the way–*sploosh!*–
the little bear was sprayed with cold water from the
elephant's trunk!

As Mason opened his wet eyes, he saw the
elephant stick his trunk in the bucket again.

Oh, no! He's getting a refill, the little bear
thought. The trunk began to rise, and Mason
couldn't help but frown.

Thinking quickly, Mason ran around the elephant and slipped his wet body through the bars of the exhibit. He was now in a tropical area full of colorful birds. That was a close call!

Mason wasn't sure how long half an hour was, but he thought maybe it had passed.

I really have to get back to Jacob before he leaves without me, he thought. But the little bear didn't know where he was, which meant he didn't know how to get back to the seal show. It looked like Mason was in a sticky situation.

Just then, Mason spotted a large, beautiful flamingo balanced on one leg.

"Excuse me," he said, "but I must get back to my friend, Jacob, right away! Would you be able to direct me to the seal show?"

"I can do better than that," the bird replied. "Hop on! The next flight leaves now!"

The little bear carefully climbed up on the bird's back and held on tight. They flew straight up into the blue sky and a warm breeze lifted them high into the air. Mason couldn't believe his eyes!

They soared over the tropical birds, the elephants, and the monkeys. By the time they flew over the seal show, Mason's fur was dry again.

The flamingo sat the little bear gently on the ground, waved goodbye, and flew away. Mason felt very grateful.

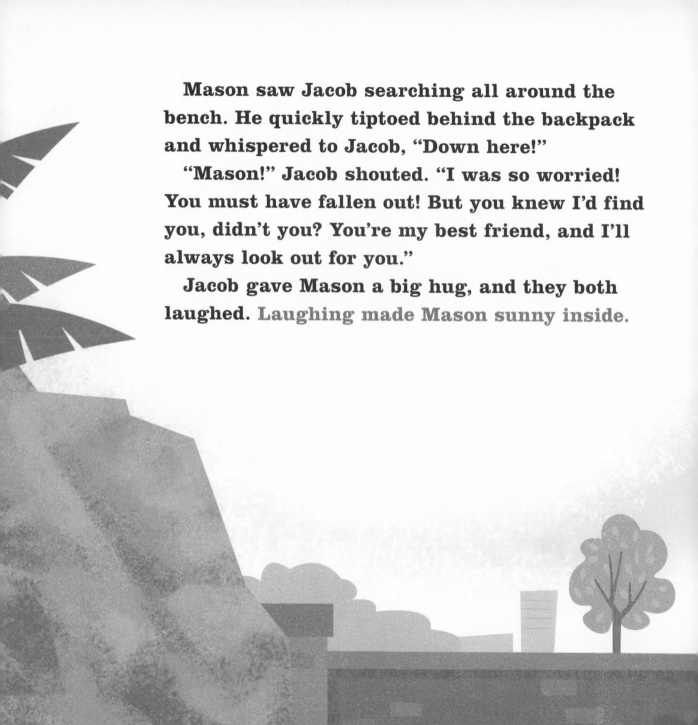

Mason saw Jacob searching all around the bench. He quickly tiptoed behind the backpack and whispered to Jacob, "Down here!"

"Mason!" Jacob shouted. "I was so worried! You must have fallen out! But you knew I'd find you, didn't you? You're my best friend, and I'll always look out for you."

Jacob gave Mason a big hug, and they both laughed. Laughing made Mason sunny inside.

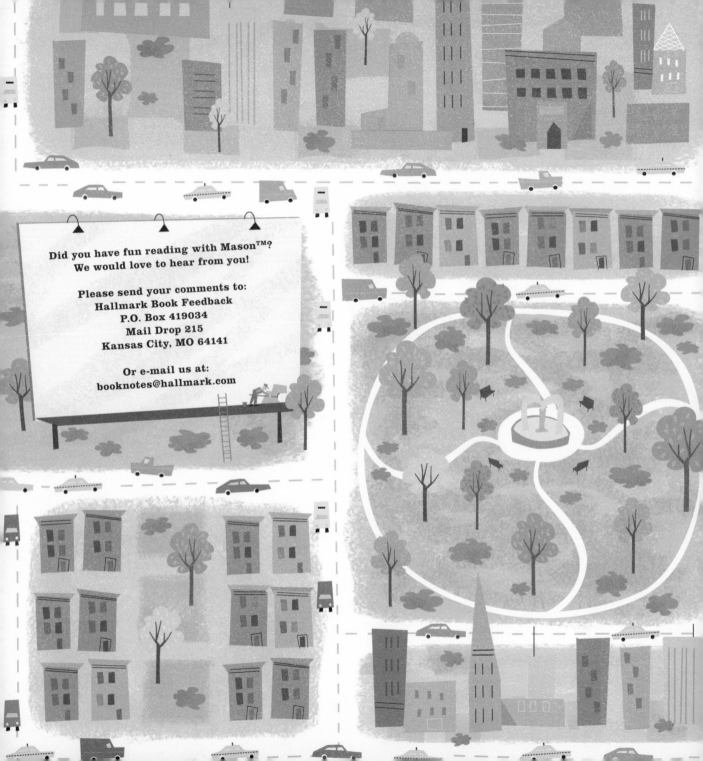

Did you have fun reading with Mason™?
We would love to hear from you!

Please send your comments to:
Hallmark Book Feedback
P.O. Box 419034
Mail Drop 215
Kansas City, MO 64141

Or e-mail us at:
booknotes@hallmark.com